To Britany,
who never forgets
how to dance in the storm.

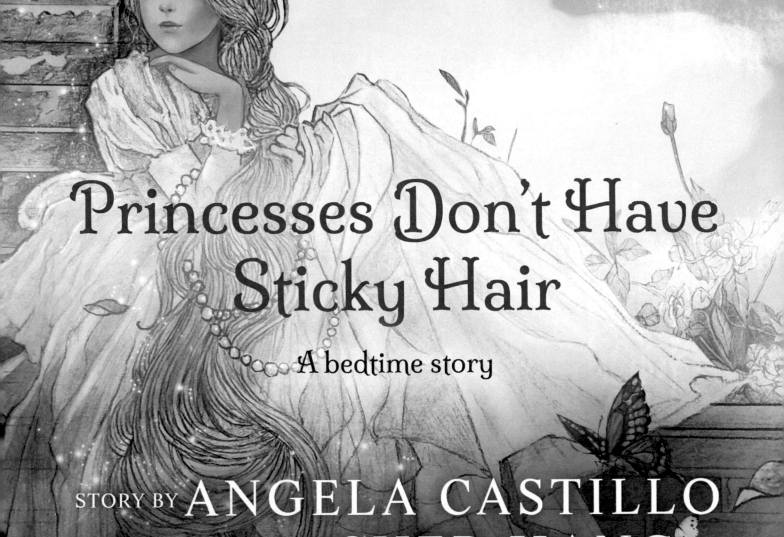

Princesses Don't Have Sticky Hair

A bedtime story

STORY BY **ANGELA CASTILLO**

ILLUSTRATED BY **CHER JIANG**

This book belongs to:

_____

Princesses don't have sticky hair . . .

unless they decide to explore a cave
and accidentally walk through
a spider web.

Dragons don't breathe fire

around company . . .

unless a friend needs

a marshmallow toasted.

Mermaids don't venture out
on dry land . . .

unless their friends

        are having a tea party.

Unicorns don't wear rain boots . . .

unless they're splashing in

mud puddles.

Fairies don't do homework . . .

unless they're practicing for
a 'spelling' test.

Brownies don't like

       making a mess . . .

except on forest art day.

Children don't like going to bed . . .

unless they have a
bedtime story.

The End

About the Author

ANGELA CASTILLO HAS BEEN WRITING STORIES SINCE she created her first book with a green crayon at the age of eight. She's lived all over Central Texas, but mostly hovered in and around the small town of Bastrop, Texas, which she loves with unnatural fierceness and features in many of her books. Angela has four wild children, a husband who studies astrophysics for fun, and a cat.

Angela's children's books can be found on Amazon in paperback and Kindle. To find out more about her books, and to download free activity pages, go to www.angelacastillowrites.weebly.com.

Other Books by Angela Castillo

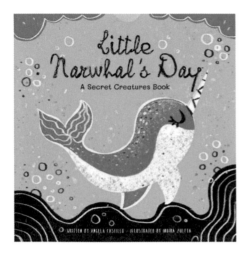

Little Narwhal's Day

Isadorn the Unicorn and the Sloppy Dragon

Tigers Can't Open Doors

Explore the secret creatures of the Arctic Circle along with Little Narwhal and his friend, Little Beluga. Bright pictures and fun characters capture the imagination while teaching about animals of the snow and ice.

Age level: 2 - 6

Dunfer the Dragon has just moved into the cave next door, and Isadorn's perfect world has been turned upside down. Includes tips to help children learn about healthy boundaries and conflict resolution.

Age level: 4 - 7

Two boys have to use their creativity to evade a goofy, shape-shifting monster. Can they do it, or will they need help from mom? Teach kids about the power of creativity and the importance of asking for help.

Age level: 3 - 7

Made in the USA
Las Vegas, NV
20 July 2021